Birthday Surprise!

Written by Milo Ferreira

Illustrated by Alison Atkins

Licensed exclusively to Top That Publishing Ltd
Tide Mill Way, Woodbridge, Suffolk, IP12 1AP, UK
www.topthatpublishing.com
Copyright © 2013 Tide Mill Media
All rights reserved
2 4 6 8 9 7 5 3 1
Manufactured in China

Written by Milo Ferreira
Illustrated by Alison Atkins

ISBN 978-1-78244-353-7

A catalogue record for this book is available from the British Library

It was another beautiful
day and Donkey was
resting in the shade
of his favourite tree.

'Hello, Tortoise. What are you doing here?' asked Donkey.

'It's a lovely day, Donkey, and I'm just out for a stroll,' replied Tortoise.

Turning around, Donkey saw another visitor.

'What are you doing in my field today, Rabbit?' asked Donkey.

'I'm practising my hopping, Donkey,' replied Rabbit.

'Here comes Cow!' said Donkey.
'What's she doing out of her barn?'

'Hello, Donkey,' said Cow. 'I'm looking for some lovely clover to eat. Have you seen any?'

'Oooh, there flies Crow,' said Donkey.

'Oh, hello, Donkey. Fancy seeing you here,' said Crow, landing in the tree.

Next to arrive were Mouse and Ratty.
'Hello, everyone!' said Mouse.

'We're looking for Badger.
Have you seen him?' asked Ratty.

'Here I am!' said Badger,
shuffling out of a hole
under Donkey's tree.

Bounding over the hill
came the farmer's new
puppy, barking at the
top of his voice.

'Why are you making
all that noise?' asked Donkey.

'Woof!' replied the puppy.
'I'm looking for the
beautiful butterfly.'

The surprises kept coming.
No sooner had Mole arrived
than the Sheep Twins came along.

'Hello,' they said together.
'Hee-haw,' said Donkey.

'Look!' said Donkey. 'Here comes the farmer chugging up the hill on his tractor. What a busy day it is today.'

As the farmer drew closer,
Donkey realised that something
special was happening.
It was Donkey's birthday!
He'd completely forgotten!
The farmer had brought a
delicious birthday cake
with him.

Everyone sang,
'Happy Birthday to you,
Happy Birthday to you,
Happy Birthday dear Donkey,
Happy Birthday to you!'